What can Pinky see?

flutter
flutter

Lucy Cousins

CANDLEWICK PRESS
CAMBRIDGE, MASSACHUSETTS

This is Pinky.
He wears glasses
so he can see
well.

What can Pinky see swimming in the pond?

splish splash

What can Pinky see in the grass?

rustle   rustle

What can pinky see in the stable?

hee
haw

What can Pinky see in the hutch?

What can Pinky see in the sky at bedtime?

twinkle   twinkle

tweet   tweet